Paul Bunyan

Retold by Rose Lewis
Illustrated by Ann Caranci

Contents

- Chapter 1 -
Paul Bunyan the Baby

Paul Bunyan was the largest baby
ever born. It took five storks
to deliver Paul to his mother and father.
"Isn't he a beautiful baby?"
asked Paul's mother.

"Yes," said Paul's father,
"but he's so big!"

Baby Paul was very hungry.
He opened up his mouth
and gave a loud cry.
His cries were so loud,
they frightened all the frogs
out of the pond.

"He's big and very loud,"
said Paul's father.

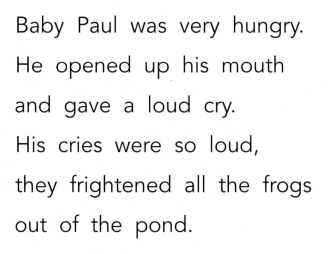

Baby Paul grew and grew.
By the time he was two weeks old,
he weighed 100 pounds.

For breakfast each morning,
Paul ate 5 dozen eggs,
20 bowls of porridge, and 30 pancakes.

There were no baby clothes that fit Paul.
Paul wore his father's shirts and pants,
but as he grew, they became too small.
Paul's mother sewed him
a giant suit of clothes.
There were no buttons
large enough for the suit,
so Paul's mother
used wagon wheels instead.

When Paul was nine months old,
he started to crawl, and that is
when the real problems began.
Paul now weighed over 500 pounds
and every time he moved,
the ground shook. He loved trees
and he would pick them
out of people's yards.
Soon, he had made a pile of trees
that was taller than a mountain.

"He can't keep picking people's trees,"
said Paul's father. "We'll have to move."

▪ Chapter 2 ▪
Paul and the Blue Ox

Paul and his family moved
to the deep forest
where there were many trees.
No one minded Paul
picking a few here and there.

Paul loved living in the woods.
He was friends with all the animals.
He could run faster than the deer
and was stronger than the bears.

maa-maa!

One cold winter day,

it snowed and snowed.

It was so cold, the snow was blue!

When Paul went outside to get some

logs for a fire, he heard a sound,

"Maa-maa!"

"Who's there?" called Paul.
He walked around looking
in the deep, blue snow.

"Maa-maa!" came the cries again.

Suddenly, Paul saw a small tail
sticking out of the snow.
He pulled on the tail
and out popped a large baby ox.
The ox was blue like the snow
and had large, white horns.

"Maa-maa!" cried the blue ox.

Paul carried the baby ox home.
"Don't worry. You will soon
be warm here," he told the ox,
and he placed the ox
by the warm fire.
The ox licked Paul's face
with his tongue. Paul laughed happily.

Paul named the ox Babe.
Babe and Paul were best friends
and went everywhere together.
Babe grew to be big and strong.

· Chapter 3 ·
Paul the Lumberjack

Paul loved living in the forest
with his mother and father,
but as he got older,
he began to think about
what he was going to do.

Paul said goodbye to his parents
and headed west. Across the country,
there were many tall trees
and people needed the trees
to build houses.

"Babe," he told his ox,
"we are going to log these trees
for people to build houses."

"Timber!" shouted Paul
as he took his ax
and cut down ten large trees
with one chop.
He loaded up the trees
onto Babe's back and then
took the trees to the sawmill
where they were made into lumber.

15

Paul and Babe traveled
all over the country clearing trees
so farmers could plant corn
and wheat and build barns.

"You know Babe, I'm getting a bit tired,"
Paul told his ox one day.
"Let's hire some fellows to help us."

Paul put up signs everywhere that said,
"Loggers needed."
Soon the word spread.

Paul wanted the biggest
and strongest men for his logging camp,
which he called the Big Onion Logging
Company. Soon Paul had hired
over 1,000 men. He built a gigantic camp
with bunkhouses and a table so long,
it took a week to pass
the salt and pepper from one end
to the other.

The cook came to Paul and said,
"We have a problem.
I can't cook enough flapjacks
to keep all these hungry men happy.
I don't have a griddle pan big enough!"

So Paul built the cook a griddle pan
the size of a lake.
The kitchen helpers greased the pan
by skating around the griddle with slabs
of bacon strapped to their feet.

The next winter lasted for two years.
One of the men came to Paul and said,
"Boss, we have trouble. The fellows
are getting frostbite when they
go out to work because it's so cold!"

"Hmmm," said Paul. "Well, tell them
to let their whiskers grow.
When their beards get to their feet,
they can knit them into socks!"

Paul, his blue ox, Babe,
and Paul's lumberjacks logged
up and down the country
for many years. They logged
all the trees in Minnesota, Washington,
Oregon, and even Alaska.
Some say that Paul and Babe are still
out there logging somewhere
around the Arctic Circle.